ANIMAL RESCUE

The Lost Duckling

This series is for my ~~...~~ who cares about all animals.

STRIPES PUBLISHING
An imprint of the Little Tiger Group
1 The Coda Centre, 189 Munster Road, London SW6 6AW

A paperback original
First published in Great Britain in 2008
This edition published in 2017

Text copyright © Jenny Oldfield, 2008, 2017
Inside illustrations copyright © Artful Doodlers, 2017
Cover illustration copyright © Anna Chernyshova, 2017
Images courtesy of www.shutterstock.com

ISBN: 978-1-84715-784-3

ANiMAL RESCUE

The Lost Duckling

TINA NOLAN

Stripes

ANIMAL MAGIC

🏠 HOME

💙 ADOPT

✋ FRIEND

RESCUE CENTRE

MEET THE ANIMALS IN NEED OF A HOME!

CLEO

A brown and white springer spaniel, 12 months old. Great with children. Loves long walks and swimming!

HUGO

A friendly, neutered brown rabbit. Litter-trained and likes a cuddle. Can you give him a home?

ROSIE

Good things come in small packages! A fab kiddies' pony with a calm temperament and gorgeous brown eyes!

  SITE SEARCH 🔍

NEWS

HELP US

CONTACT

£ **DONATE!**

VAL

An old lady and a total darling. This golden Labrador will do anything for you. Can you give her a loving home?

MICKEY

OK, so he's loud! But Mickey wouldn't hurt a fly. A nosey, lovable donkey in need of a big field and caring owners.

BLOSSOM

A good-looking feline found wandering on the wild side. Lots of TLC needed to turn Blossom into the ideal pet.

Chapter One

"'Spring into Action!' – I've always liked that," Mark Harrison said. "It's a great slogan for Animal Magic. 'Spring into Action!' – it sounds very positive."

"Thanks," Karl said, staring longingly at his pizza.

The Harrisons – Mark, Heidi, Karl and Eva – plus Joel, Animal Magic's veterinary assistant, were celebrating at the best Italian restaurant in town.

"Hey, Karl!" Eva objected. "I helped

you think of it, remember!"

"Spring into Action" – the springtime slogan for the rescue centre – had worked wonders, and it was partly down to Eva and her brother Karl working on the website together.

And right now the family had another reason to celebrate. "This is the time to look forward," Heidi reminded them.

Mark nodded. "Absolutely! The Council finally said no to Linda's petition to have us closed down."

"Let's drink to that!" Joel said.

"And look at how well we've been doing recently," Heidi added. "Since early May we've found good homes for 18 out of the 20 dogs we've rescued, 12 out of 15 cats, six out of six hamsters, besides all the other small animals that have been brought in – rabbits, ferrets, mice – you name it, we've rehomed it!"

"We're on a roll," Mark agreed. "I think the spring campaign is really working."

"Yes!" Heidi said, raising her glass.

Eva and Karl didn't need to be told twice. They tucked into their pizzas and chomped quietly.

"Ah, peace!" Mark joked. "I have found, over the years, that food is the only thing that keeps you two quiet."

Chewy, crusty pizza with slurpy tomato sauce, pepperoni and melted cheese on top – yum! Eva munched in silence.

"Which gives me the chance to say thanks to everyone for all the effort you put in to keeping Animal Magic open," Heidi went on. "It's been a stressful time, waiting for the Council to consider Linda's petition, but you all worked your socks off to make sure we got the right decision."

Joel, Eva and Karl grinned and nodded.

"Finally!" Karl mumbled between mouthfuls.

"We won. Nothing can stop us now!"

Eva smiled. "Whatever Linda Brooks says, we can rescue animals and match the perfect pet with the perfect owner *forever* – can't we, Dad?"

"You bet," Mark said, giving first Eva then Karl a high five. Then he snuck a look at Heidi and Joel – a look which seemed to say, "Don't spoil the moment – let them enjoy it" – and the two grown-ups nodded back at him and drank from their glasses. Then Heidi called for the pudding menu.

"Sticky toffee," Eva decided. "With ice cream."

"Please," Mark reminded her.

"Please!"

"Double chocolate fudge cake with chocolate sauce." Karl chose carefully from the list.

"Pl—" Mark began.

"Please!"

The waiter grinned as he took the order. "Looks like someone's celebrating," he said when he came back with their puddings.

Everybody nodded happily.

Munch-munch – seriously sticky, totally toffee – Eva was in dessert heaven! "I've got another wicked idea for the website," she announced between gulps. "We should do a spring-clean-for-pets information thing – you know, how to get rid of fleas and tapeworms and stuff."

"Please!" Joel groaned. "Not while we're eating."

"Cool," Karl said. "Did you know a single flea can lay up to 27 eggs per day? We could give lots of info on how to get rid of them."

"Yuck, it's making me itch just thinking about it." But Joel knew when he was beaten by this animal-mad family. He fell silent and tucked into his strawberry ice cream.

Heidi nodded. "You two can do the research then run it past me before you put it on the site."

"Brilliant!" Karl high-fived Eva.

"We'll do it tomorrow!" she said with a grin.

Chapter Two

Next morning, a Saturday, Eva was up early.

"Come on, Cleo, let's go for a walk," she said to the young springer spaniel, who was raring to go.

Cleo jumped up at her kennel door. Along the row, other puppies and dogs wagged their tails and woofed.

"Later, Mitch. Soon, Val," Eva told the yappy Jack Russell and the elderly golden Labrador. "I'll take you two for a walk after I've been down to the river with Cleo."

She slid the bolt to Cleo's door and the spaniel leaped out, racing down the aisle and bouncing up at the door that led out into the yard. "Slow down," Eva said with a shake of her head. She needed to get the dog on the lead in case she raced out on to the road. "What's the hurry, Cleo?"

The spaniel jumped up, long ears flopping, short tail wagging.

"Sit!" Eva ordered. "Good girl." Quickly she clipped the lead on to Cleo's collar. "OK, now we can go."

Closing the door on the other dogs, Eva set off for the river. She held Cleo on a tight lead out of the yard and on to Okeham Main Street. Just past the house they took a left down the side of Animal Magic along an overgrown path leading to a stile and a footpath across fields to the nearby river. At the stile it was safe for Cleo to run free, so Eva let her off the lead.

"Wow, she sure can sprint!" she murmured as the dog bounded off through the long grass. "Heel, Cleo!" she called, seeing a young rabbit shoot out across the path with Cleo hard on its heels.

The spaniel obeyed, ears drooping, tail tucked between her legs.

"Good girl," Eva told her. "No chasing poor, teeny-weeny baby rabbits, OK?"

They walked on for a while in the early morning sun. Blackbirds trilled in the hawthorn hedges, pigeons cooed from the nearby woods.

Soon Eva could hear the sound of water rippling over a stony bed, and when they turned the corner they came out along the bank where the river bent in a wide arc. Nearby there was an old stone bridge and the smooth expanse of the golf course beyond.

"OK, Cleo, now you can go and play," Eva said, pointing to a pebble bank and the cool, clear water.

With a yelp of joy Cleo went flying down to the river, nose down, following every delicious scent of the early summer morning. She sniffed here and there, at rabbit holes, molehills and patches

of scuffed earth, seizing a stick and
bringing it to Eva, then darting back
and waiting for it to be thrown.

"Fetch!" Eva called, flinging the stick
as far as she could into the river.

The little spaniel plunged in and
doggy-paddled towards the floating
stick. She snatched at it and brought it
back to shore.

"Hey!" Eva yelped as she bent to pick
up the stick. Cleo had just shaken herself
from top to toe. Icy droplets soaked Eva
to the skin. But she threw the stick a
second time and watched.

Cleo swam with her head just clear
of the sparkling surface. She was three
or four metres from the stick, which
was floating slowly downstream, when
suddenly Eva saw the ducklings.

"Oh!" she said out loud, as the four little ducks paddled midstream. One after the other, they swam in a line – fluffy and yellow, heads up, battling the current. "Sweet!"

But where are their mum and dad? Eva wondered.

Woof! Spotting the ducklings, Cleo changed course and swam straight towards them.

Uh-oh! "Here, Cleo – heel!" Eva called.

This time the eager spaniel ignored her and made a beeline for the ducklings.

They were swimming against the current, too tiny to make much headway and scared stiff by the creature with the broad head and sharp white teeth that drew nearer and nearer. *Cheep!* they cried. *Cheep-cheep!*

"Cleo, come back!" Eva shouted.

Just then the ducklings' parents appeared from under the shelter of the far bank. They swam rapidly across the water, craning their necks and quacking loudly at Cleo.

"Bad dog, Cleo!" Eva yelled.

The spaniel turned her head. The adult ducks were speeding towards her, flapping their wings, half rising out of the water like angry jet-skiers.

Good for you! Eva thought, admiring the sleek green-black head of the male duck with its bright yellow beak, and the brown speckles of the female. *You tell Cleo off as much as you like – I don't blame you!*

Cheep-cheep! the ducklings cried. In their panic, they split off in four different directions.

Quack! The mother duck called them back. Three of them turned and swam straight to join her. But the fourth and smallest duckling – a ball of yellow fluff bobbing in the middle of the river – ignored her mother's call.

Meanwhile, the drake attacked Cleo. He flew at her, flapping across the water, stabbing at her with his beak and making a terrific racket.

Woof! Suddenly Cleo didn't like the look of this. She turned away from the lonely duckling and its angry dad and began swimming back to shore.

"That's right, come here!" Eva called.

Good riddance! The male duck followed, quacking angrily. Then, when he was sure Cleo had backed down, he turned and began to shoo the fourth, dithery duckling towards her brothers and sisters.

Cheep! The tiny cry sounded so cute.

Quack! said the angry dad.

"Thank goodness!" Eva sighed with relief to see the family back together. "Don't tell the little one off. She might be a bit scatty, but she was confused and didn't know what to do when big bad Cleo suddenly appeared!"

Then, as quickly as the danger had begun, it was over. The spaniel was back onshore, shaking herself and drenching Eva. "Bad girl!" Eva said again.

Cleo hung her head and tucked her tail between her legs.

Meanwhile, the four yellow ducklings were swimming with their parents towards the far bank. All was well.

"Dilly, Dilly duckling!" Eva made up a song as they walked back across the fields. "Bright yellow daffy-dilly, dizzy little thing!" *Yeah*, she thought, *Dilly!*

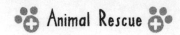

Dilly's a good name for the scatty one!
She climbed the stile and walked
rapidly up the footpath. *I can't wait to tell
everyone about Cleo and Dilly the duckling!*

Chapter Three

"Oh no, Eva's already given the duckling a name!" Karl scoffed. "She's called it Dilly and now she's in *lurve* – again!"

"I am not!" Eva retorted. She'd been in the surgery, telling her mum all about the ducklings when her brother interrupted.

"Are!"

"Am not!"

"Hush, you two!" Heidi warned, picking up the phone. "OK, Cath, I can hear you now – yes, we do have a spare stable, we could take Rosie any time that suits you … yes, straight away then..OK, bye!"

"I only said Dilly was cute!" Eva protested. "She's the littlest one, and she got separated from the others. Her big brave dad looked after her though."

"How do you even know it's a she?" Karl asked. While Eva had been out with Cleo, he'd been looking up flea facts and writing pages for the website. He'd discovered that fleas feed on blood. They lay eggs which drop from your pet on to the carpet and furniture. "Did you know fleas prefer temperatures between 18 and 23 degrees?" he added.

"Yeah, I really needed to know that," Eva huffed. If Karl wasn't going to show

any interest in her ducklings, no way was
she going to get excited about fleas.

"Mum, how many ducklings usually
hatch out in one nest?"

"Maybe six or seven," Heidi said
absent-mindedly. She was busy jotting
down lists of figures in a notebook. "Not
all survive though."

"What happens to the ones who don't?"

"Oh, they're taken by foxes perhaps.
Or else they get separated from the rest
before they're big enough to feed and
look after themselves. There are loads
of deadly dangers out there for a little
duckling."

Eva shuddered. "Well anyway, Dilly
got safely back to her family before
Cleo could do anything horrid, thank
heavens."

Heidi nodded.

"Dilly!" Karl snorted, going back to his flea info.

"Eva, take Cleo into the kennels and give her a good rub down with a towel. Then, if you like, you could come back and help me here." Heidi closed her notebook and put on her pale-blue surgery tunic. She looked at her watch. "Almost time for the mad rush."

"I was going to take Mitch and Val for a walk," Eva told her.

"Oh yeah, any excuse to go back and see the fluffy-wuffy ickle ducklings!" Karl grunted without turning round.

"Well, I don't mind," Heidi shrugged. "But I thought you'd like to help me admit Rosie."

"Who's Rosie?" Eva asked.

"Rosie is a twelve-year-old Shetland pony who's looking for a home. I just took a phone call about her from Cath Brown at Leebank Pony Sanctuary. Cath rescued her a few weeks back from a deserted caravan site just outside the city. From what she told me, the poor thing was practically starving."

"And is she OK now?" Eva asked, all thoughts of another dog walk, fleas and ducklings quickly biting the dust.

Heidi nodded. "Cath fed her up and got her back into good condition. Now she wants to hand her over to us. I said we'd rehome Rosie, no problem."

"Cool!" Eva cried. "Which stable shall we put her in? Shall I lay a bed of fresh straw? Do Shetlands need special feed? What colour is she?"

"Whoa!" Heidi laughed. "You can prepare the end stable next to Mickey the donkey if you like. And you can get Annie to help you."

Through the window Heidi had spotted Annie Brooks running across the yard. Annie burst in through the door. "Hi, Heidi, Hi, Karl! Eva, do you want to come and ride Guinevere with me?"

"Sorry, Annie, I'm too busy," Eva replied hurriedly. "We've got a new pony coming in." She disappeared down the corridor to dry Cleo and put her into her kennel. When she came back, Annie was hovering behind Karl, reading his newly created web page.

"Yuck!" Annie said. "Ewww! Fleas are attracted by your pet's body heat and movement. You can get skin diseases from them!"

"Enough about fleas!" Eva protested. "Annie, do you want to help me sort out the stable…?"

"You bet!" Annie replied, racing out of Reception ahead of Eva. "What kind of pony? When? What's its name?"

"A Shetland. Now. Rosie," Eva replied.

"Exciting!" Annie said.

Soon the girls were cutting the strings around a bale of straw and scattering the bedding. In the stable next door, Mickey scuffled his feet.

Karl had given him his full name, Mickey Mouse, when he arrived at Animal Magic. "His coat is mouse colour, and he's got big ears. And anyway, Mickey Mouse suits him."

"Who says?" Eva had quizzed.

"I do," Karl had replied.

"It's OK, Mickey, calm down," Eva soothed now. "You're going to have a new neighbour – someone you'll like, I promise!" She hung up a hay net, checked the water supply and the light switch. Everything was in working order.

"So when can we ride Guinevere?" Annie wanted to know, when the bed was laid. She was eager to go out on her mum's lovely grey mare.

"After Rosie gets here," Eva decided. "I can bring Val and Mitch with me and you can ride down the path to the river. With a bit of luck, we'll see Dilly."

Annie rested against the stable door. "Dilly who?" she asked.

And Eva was off again – "Dilly duckling – yellow and fluffy – *cheep-cheep* – so cute!"

It was almost midday before Cath drove her trailer into the yard at Animal Magic. Meanwhile, Eva and Annie had been helping Joel in the surgery.

"What can we do while we're waiting for Rosie?" Eva had asked.

"Plenty. You can wipe down the treatment tables for a start," Joel had said. Then he'd admitted a rabbit and told Eva to give Karl information for the website.

"Hugo – a friendly, neutered brown rabbit. Litter-trained and likes a cuddle," Eva dictated.

Karl had typed fast while Annie had taken a photo of the new admission.

Then they'd taken in a feral cat, found near the cricket pavilion and brought in by the team captain, plus an unwanted hamster. The morning had flown.

"Here comes the Leebank trailer!" Karl called just before twelve o'clock.

"At last!" Eva and Annie rushed out to greet it.

Cath stepped down from her Land

Rover. "Sorry I took so long," she apologized. "One of the ponies got a touch of colic. I had to call the vet."

"Can we see Rosie?" Eva asked, jumping up and down with excitement.

Cath grinned. "Stand well back while I lower the ramp and lead her out."

By this time, Heidi, Joel and Karl had come out of the surgery and Mark had strolled out of the house, so there was a small crowd to meet the new arrival.

They waited on tenterhooks until Cath emerged from the trailer, then there were gasps and soft cries of surprise.

"Oh, she's so small!"

"Tiny!"

"Sweet!"

Cath led Rosie down the ramp. The little Shetland was chocolate brown with

a white flash on her nose and two white
forelegs. Her heavy brown mane hung
long and shaggy over her face and neck;
her legs were short and stumpy.

"Nice fat belly," Heidi said with a grin.
"Definitely no sign of her starving now!"

"Look at her little hooves!" Annie cried.

"Such a cute face!" Eva sighed.

Even Karl joined in. "Yep, she's cool," he agreed. "I reckon she's about as big as a Great Dane."

"Smaller!" Annie insisted. "Tiny, tiny!"

"Eva, would you lead her to her stable?" Cath asked, handing over the rope.

Slowly and gently, Eva led Rosie into her new home. The others followed.

An inquisitive Mickey stuck his big, bony head over his door and stared down at Rosie. *Ee-aw!*

Rosie walked on by without a sideways glance. She'd smelled sweet hay in the hay net and fresh, clean straw.

"She's pretty calm and relaxed considering how badly she's been treated," Cath advised. "And of course she'll make a wonderful kiddies' pony. You should put that in your advert."

Ee-aw! Mickey insisted from next door.

Rosie took no notice and got stuck in to her hay – *munch-munch.*

"We'll put her on the website right away," Heidi told Cath. "And we'll let you know as soon as we find a good owner for her."

Munch-munch. Rosie rolled the hay around her mouth and ground it between her teeth.

Ee-aw! Mickey brayed.

Mark put his hands over his ears. "What a racket! I'm out of here!"

"Me too," Joel agreed.

Gradually the stables emptied, until only Eva and Annie were left. The two girls stared at Rosie with total delight.

"So shall we ride Guinnie now?" Annie said at last.

"If we can tear ourselves away," Eva answered dreamily. She loved Rosie's dark brown eyes peering out from under the shaggy fringe.

"Guinnie needs the exercise," Annie reminded Eva.

"And I ought to walk Val and Mitch," Eva sighed. *If only Mum would let me keep Rosie!* But no, she knew that would never happen.

It was Annie's turn to sigh. "Come on then – let's go."

"Yes, let's go."

They sighed again, but for the longest time neither Eva nor Annie moved.

Chapter Four

"Steady, Guinevere, no need to barge."
Annie reined her horse back to let Eva
open the gate. The two dogs, Mitch
and Val, ran ahead.

It was half past twelve and at last
the two girls had torn themselves away
from gorgeous Rosie.

"Lunch is at one-thirty!" Linda
Brooks had called over the fence as
she heard Annie set off for the river on
Guinevere. "Don't be late!"

They had an hour to walk the dogs, exercise Guinevere and look for the ducklings.

"Go ahead, canter Guinnie around the edge of the field," Eva told Annie as she shut the gate. "I'll catch you up down by the river."

She led the dogs on a short cut and arrived ahead of Annie, holding open the next gate and letting them through.

"Your turn." Annie dismounted and offered Eva her hard hat.

Quickly, Eva slid her foot in the stirrup and swung into the saddle. With a click of her tongue she headed the grey mare along the riverside path. "The ducklings were a bit further along, round that bend in the river," she explained to Annie, who called Val and Mitch and put them on the lead.

Leading the way, Eva kept her eyes peeled. "Watch out for the golfers!" she called over her shoulder. Across the river, a player struck a ball high into the air and Eva watched it plop safely on to the green.

Val and Mitch barked at the ball, desperate to chase after it.

"Sorry you two," Annie said. "You've

got to stay on your leads."

"The ducklings were around here somewhere, swimming in the middle of the river," Eva told Annie. "I can't see them yet – no, they're not here – oh yes, there they are!"

Sure enough, a family of baby ducks appeared at the edge of the river, paddling amongst the eddies, while two adults swam further out from the bank, keeping a careful lookout.

"One, two, three, four … five!" Eva counted the ducklings. She looked again. "Hey, this must be a different family. Yes, the ducklings are bigger, which means they're a bit older than the ones I saw this morning. They've got more brown speckles…"

"They're still cute," Annie said with

a smile. She kept tight hold of the dogs and watched the ducklings splash and dive. "Look at that one chasing after its mother. Its little legs are paddling like crazy!"

"But where's Dilly?" Eva wondered. "If you saw her, you'd really be talking cute!"

Walking Gumme slowly along the riverbank, she kept a lookout for her first and favourite duckling family. She saw a tiny black and white dipper skim the surface of the sparkling water, then veer off towards the golf course.

"Hey, Eva!" Annie called, pointing to the far bank. "Is that them?"

And there they were – four little yellow ducklings following their sleek brown mother up the steep bank on to the smooth grass of the golf course.

The mum waddled ahead, her flat, webbed feet placed firmly on the ground. The little ones followed, stopping and starting, lowering their heads to nip at blades of grass, then scooting quickly to catch up with their mum.

"Oh yes! Look, Dilly's the little one bringing up the rear!" Eva cried, jumping down from the saddle and letting Guinevere drop her head to graze. "Uh-oh, she can't get up the slope – oh yes, she can – go on, Dilly, you can make it!"

"She's getting left behind!" Annie said, willing Dilly to scramble up the bank. "Hey, wait for her!" she called to the others.

The tiny duckling struggled to catch up.

"Why are they heading over the golf course?" Annie wanted to know. "Shouldn't they stay by the river?"

Eva shrugged. "I don't know. And I don't think those golfers have seen them either. If they're not careful they'll hit the balls straight at the ducklings!"

On went the mother duck, marching across the green. One, two, three – the bigger ducklings followed. Four! Finally Dilly made it on to the golf course.

Whack! The first golfer hit a ball on to the green. *Thud!* It landed ten metres from Eva's family of ducklings. Their mother quacked and ran back to herd her offspring into a tight huddle.

"I've got to warn those men!" Eva decided. She waved her arms and shouted. "Excuse me. Can you wait a few minutes before you hit the next ball?"

The three men looked across the river
and frowned at the two girls with a
horse and two dogs. "What was that
you said?" one yelled back.

"Can you wait until the ducks have got
across the green?" Eva repeated. Then
she remembered her manners. "Please!"

"Ducks?" the same man echoed. "Where?"

"There!" Eva pointed to the mother duck and her brood. "Your golf balls are scaring them!"

The man turned to his two companions, who shook their heads and stood with hands on hips.

"Oops!" Annie muttered. "They don't look happy."

"Neither does Dilly." Eva saw her favourite duckling cower in the middle of the bunch. Then the mother duck flapped her wings and quickly began to hustle the ducklings back down towards the river.

"That's right," Annie murmured. "Get out of their way!"

"Hang on, I'm sure they won't take long!" Eva called to the golfers.

"Fancy having to stop play because of a bunch of daft ducks!" one of them grumbled.

Soon, though, the mother managed to get her ducklings across the open green and into the long grass of the riverbank.

"It's OK now!" Eva called. "Thanks!"

"Relief!" Annie sighed. "And look, here comes the dad!"

Just then a drake flew low along the course of the river. He beat his wings strongly, swooping down and landing in the water with a splash. With a loud quack he called for his family to join him. And out came the mother duck with her babies. Dilly was last as usual, cheeping and bobbing in the rough water, struggling to keep up.

"I hope Dilly doesn't get left behind again," Annie muttered, watching another family of ducks swim out from the bank.

"Oh dear, I don't think the two families get on." Eva noticed the drakes stretch out their necks and flap their wings. The females too were making a lot of fuss, leaving their babies and doing the jet-ski thing to warn each other off.

Annie looked at her watch. "Oops, it's nearly half-one. I'm going to be late. Come on, Val, up you get. Home time, Mitch!" Quickly she led the dogs back along the path.

Lingering only to make sure that Dilly had caught up with her brothers and sisters, Eva leaped on to Guinnie's back and headed for home. "What did you think of Dilly?" she called to Annie, who had hurried ahead.

"Totally cute!" Annie agreed.

Eva smiled as Guinevere trod steadily along the track. "You know what," she decided, talking more to herself than to Annie. "I'm going to write about

Dilly and her family on Animal Magic's website – where they live, what they eat, how quickly they grow up and stuff."

"A blog!" Annie nodded. "That's a great idea!"

Eva grinned and urged Guinnie on towards home. "Yes, I'm going to start an online duckling diary!"

Chapter Five

<u>Sunday, 13th.</u> Went out with Cleo twice, down to the river. Didn't see Dilly. Spotted the family of older ducklings though. Five of them with Mum. No sign of Dilly and the others, boo-hoo.

<u>Monday, 14th.</u> School today, so couldn't go down to the river until teatime. Still no Dilly duckling. Typical! Just because I decide to write this blog, she vanishes!

Eva closed the laptop and sighed. The missing duckling wasn't the only thing on her mind. Earlier that day she'd heard Mum talking to Dad – something about donations to Animal Magic being down last month and not having enough money to pay some bills. Her mum had looked worried and had stopped talking the moment she'd seen Eva.

It wasn't fair! Just when they'd received the good news from the Council, it seemed that there was something new to worry about.

<u>Tuesday. 15th.</u> No Dilly! Miss E came to Annie's house to visit Guinnie and Merlin. Hope I see Dilly tomorrow.

Late that night, tucked up in bed, Eva thought about what she'd put on her blog. It had been a busy few days at Animal Magic. Blossom the feral cat had been quickly rehomed. Three people had already been to look at Rosie. A family called Whitaker said they were very interested in offering her a home. Mitch the terrier had been taken in by the local joiner, Pete Knight, one of the volunteers who had helped her dad build the stable block.

So Eva hadn't had much time to look for Dilly or to keep a record in her blog.

"Anyway, there's nothing to write about!" she sighed as she settled down to sleep. She lay awake for a while, thinking of little Dilly bobbing on the water and remembering what her mum

had said a few days before. "Not all
ducklings survive… They're taken by
foxes … or they get separated … there
are a hundred deadly dangers out there
for a little duckling."

What if Dilly has got lost?

"Still awake?" Heidi asked, popping
her head round Eva's door when she
came up to bed herself.

Eva nodded.

Her mum came to sit on the edge of
her bed. "Worried about something?"

"I haven't seen Dilly for ages," Eva
confessed. "The last time was when
I was with Annie and some golfers
nearly whacked their ball straight at
the ducklings! Plus, there was another
family of ducks, and the grown-ups were
arguing, plus…"

"Whoa!" Heidi shushed her. "Listen, ducks are territorial. They like to have their own stretch of riverbank, or an area on a pond, like most other animals. If there's more than one family by the bridge, it's likely that one has been chased off elsewhere. That's probably what's happened to Dilly and her family."

Eva listened and nodded. "That's most likely the reason why the mother duck was herding Dilly and the others up the bank over the golf course – she was looking for somewhere else to live."

"Exactly. Which is the reason you haven't seen Dilly lately," her mum agreed.

"But what if she got left behind?" Eva said, still worried. "I mean, she's so little and she could easily get separated and lost…"

Heidi shook her head. "I think you're worrying more than you need. Dilly is probably safe with her family, tucked away in a nice new stretch of riverbank, and busily settling into her new home!"

Deciding to extend her search next day, Eva lay for a while in silence.

"Mum," she said after a while.

"Mmm?"

"What were you and Dad talking about yesterday – you know, something to do with money and stuff?"

"Nothing for you to worry about," Heidi replied, gently patting Eva's hand.

"Is it about Animal Magic?" Eva persisted. "Are we running out of money to run our rescue centre?"

"Sshh!" Heidi stroked Eva's hair back from her face. "Money is always a struggle, it's true. We're a charity, so we rely on gifts and voluntary contributions. But you and Karl have to let me and your dad look after that side of things. That's what we grown-ups do!"

Slowly, Eva nodded. "Mum…" she began after another long pause. She was feeling sleepy at last, drifting off, with just one more question to ask.

"Yes?"

"If we run out of money, will we have to close Animal Magic, even though we got the good news from the Council?"

"Sshh!" Heidi replied. "Go to sleep, there's a good girl."

<u>Wednesday, 16th.</u> Walked over the old bridge and searched further down the riverbank. Still no Dilly! Am worried, even though Mum said not to be. Where is she? Is she lost and all alone? What happened to her and her family?
The Whitaker family said no to Rosie in the end because it turns out they might have to move house.
Dilly, Dilly, where are you?

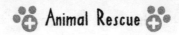

On the Thursday afternoon Eva had come out of school with a load of homework. But instead of getting the bus as usual, her dad had picked her and Karl up in his delivery van and driven them home.

"Good day?" Mark had asked, and Karl had told him that Jake Harwood's mum had said yes to Ernie the hamster and they were coming to Animal Magic to see him straight after school.

Eva sat quietly, staring out of the window as the houses of the city gradually gave way to fields. *Maths homework – yuck! English – read chapters six and seven of the class reader.*

Walk Val before tea. Walk Cleo after.

Look for Dilly again.

"Eva?" Mark asked. "Hey, daydreamer, did you hear what I just said?"

Eva gave a small start. She recognized the edge of Okeham village – they were passing the end of Earlswood Avenue, then Swallow Court. "What? No."

"I said that the sale of Miss Eliot's old house, Ash Tree Manor, has just gone through. She called in at the rescue centre earlier today to tell Mum."

"Is that good?" Eva asked. She remembered the time when Karl had climbed a tree in the garden of Miss Eliot's ancient manor house and rescued the old lady's tabby cat, Tigger.

Soon after that, Miss Eliot had decided the house was too much for her and had moved to her bungalow in Swallow Court. Animal Magic had taken in her pregnant grey mare, Guinevere, which was where her lovely foal, Merlin, had been born. Then bossy Linda Brooks had fallen in love with Guinevere and Merlin and she'd forgiven Animal Magic for all the animal noises and extra traffic they'd brought to the village.

"It's *very* good news," Mark told Eva now. "I'm happy for her. Miss Eliot is relieved it's all over and she has the money from the sale of the manor. No more money worries for that old lady, at least."

"Cool," Eva said absent-mindedly. Then, as they drove up Main Street, closer to home, she suddenly yelled, "Dad, watch out! Brake, Dad, brake!"

There, right in front of them, was the last thing she'd expected to see — two ducks and four ducklings marching in single file straight across the road!

Mark glanced in his mirror then slammed on the brakes. The van swerved slightly towards the pavement then stopped. "Everyone OK?" he asked.

Karl nodded.

"It's Dilly!" Eva cried. "Look — the little one at the back. She's not lost after all — that's Dilly!"

Hop-skip-hop — the fluffy yellow bundle scrambled to keep up.

"Narrow escape," Karl muttered. "Can I get out and shoo them on to the side of the road?"

Mark gave the go-ahead. "Watch out for traffic," he warned.

Waddle-waddle – the adult ducks took no notice of the van and made their way steadily from one side of the road to the other.

Karl jumped out. "Shoo!" he called, making a whooshing, herding gesture with his arms. "Go on, shoo!"

Eva glanced anxiously up and down the road. Luckily, there were no other cars around – only George Stevens, Karl's friend, cycling by. He stopped to let Karl herd the ducks safely across the road.

"What are they doing here?" Eva asked, still hardly able to believe her eyes.

Waddle-waddle, hop-skip-hop. The road was hard, grey and wide for the tiny ducklings.

"I've no idea," Mark replied. He waited until Karl had finished the job and told George what was going on.

"We nearly ran them over!" Karl reported. "Talk about bird-brained!"

"That's not fair," Eva muttered. "You can't blame the ducks!"

"No, they don't know any better. But a busy road is a pretty dangerous place

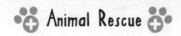

to go walkabout," her dad pointed out.
"Let's hope they don't try it again."

Eva frowned but stayed silent as Karl
jumped back in the van and her dad
drove the last few metres home. Her
head was buzzing – not about maths
or walking the dogs, it was about Dilly
and what else she, Eva, could do to
make sure Dilly and her family were
safer on the road.

Chapter Six

<u>Thursday, 17th.</u> Major traffic panic. Dilly and her family tried to cross the main road and we nearly ran them over! <u>***They're not by the riverbank any more, they're living on the big pond behind Swallow Court.***</u>
This is how I found out – Dad picked us up from school and as we drove along, they were crossing the road with Dilly lagging behind as usual. Dad braked and we missed them.
The minute we got home, I went back to look for them. I asked Miss Eliot

if she'd seen the ducklings on the road because she was sitting in her garden with Tigger when it happened. She said yes, she watched it all. Then she saw the adult ducks lead the ducklings on down the crescent. They actually crossed her garden and went into the field at the back!

So I climbed over Miss Eliot's fence and followed the ducks to the pond. It belongs to Mr and Mrs Truelove. They own a big house with a tennis court and a pond and everything – Swallow Hall.

So Dilly's got a new home, not by the river any more. And Mrs Truelove says I can visit the pond any time I like to keep an eye on her. Phew! But in any case, Karl and I decided to make a sign for the road just in case the ducks go back that way again. 'SLOW DOWN – DUCKS CROSSING!' in giant red letters.

We stuck the cardboard sign on a wooden stake and hammered it into the grass verge. Hope it works.
Didn't have time to do English homework. Hope Mum will write a note for Miss Jennings to let me off. Fingers crossed.
<u>***Dilly's safe and she's not lost. How cool is that!***</u>

"So, Rosie, I got into big trouble with Miss Jennings today," Eva told the Shetland pony. It was Friday evening, and Mickey the donkey was noisily chewing hay in the stable next door. "Mum wouldn't write me a note. She said making the DUCKS CROSSING! sign wasn't a good enough excuse for me not doing my homework. Is that mean or what!"

Rosie nuzzled Eva's hand, looking
for a treat. Her long, shaggy forelock
completely covered her eyes.

"How do you see through all that hair?" Eva wondered, gently pushing the mane to one side. "So anyway, I tried to explain, but Miss Jennings gave me a big speech about how schoolwork should always come first, no matter what. In front of the whole class! In the end she gave me extra work, which I now have to hand in, plus the homework on Monday morning!"

Life was tough, Eva decided, though Rosie didn't seem to care. Instead, she wandered over to her hay net and began to munch.

"Ah, here you are!" Miss Eliot interrupted as Eva leaned against Rosie's stable door, chin resting on the top. "Your mother said I might find you here."

Eva swung round to face the old lady.

"Why, has something happened?" she asked anxiously. "Is Dilly OK?"

"Yes, yes!" Miss Eliot smiled. "That's what I came to tell you — I was looking out of my bedroom window earlier this afternoon, and I saw the whole family swimming on the Trueloves' pond. They look as if they've settled nicely."

"That's brilliant!" Eva heaved a sigh of relief. She was grateful to Miss Eliot for coming specially to tell her. "I'd like to come down and see Dilly, if that's OK with you."

Another smile and a nod. "Of course, my dear. That's what Heidi guessed you'd say, so I told her I'd keep a careful eye on you while you take a look down by the pond."

"OK." Feeling like a little toddler in

need of a child minder, Eva went with
Miss Eliot across the yard and out on to
Main Street. Still, she knew the old lady
meant well.

"Your sign seems to be working,"
Miss Eliot pointed out as two cars
slowed down almost to a halt. "Drivers
certainly seem to be reading it."

"Cool," Eva noted. "It was my idea —
just in case the ducks try to get back to
the river."

"Very thoughtful," Miss Eliot agreed.
She and Eva passed the sign and
turned into Swallow Crescent and the
neat row of bungalows with their small
front gardens. They found Tigger sitting
patiently on the front doorstep, waiting
for his owner to return.

As Miss Eliot invited Eva into her

garden, she gave a small click of her
tongue, as if hesitating over what she
was about to say. "Tell me, dear, is your
mother well?"

The question surprised Eva. "She's
fine, thanks," she said.

"Only, she looked a little pale. And
she didn't seem her usual cheerful self,"
the old lady went on.

"She's been pretty busy," Eva
admitted, trying to scan the field at the
back of Miss Eliot's house to catch sight
of Dilly and her family on the pond.
"And she didn't get much sleep. Last
night someone rang her at midnight to
say they'd got back home from their
holiday and heard an animal whining
and growling from inside their garage.
The woman was too scared to open the

door, so Mum had to go and find out what was trapped inside.

"It turned out it was a stray dog – a cross-breed that got in and couldn't get out again. It had nearly starved to death while the woman was away. Mum brought the dog straight back to Animal Magic."

"I certainly do admire your mother," Miss Eliot told Eva. "But are you sure that nothing is worrying her?"

Eva shrugged. "Only the usual stuff about trying to pay bills and not having enough money," she admitted. "But that's nothing new for Animal Magic."

"Your mother does amazingly good work." Miss Eliot nodded her head and took a deep breath, as if she'd just come to a big decision. "Now, I expect you're wanting to go down to the pond for a

closer look at your ducklings," she said
to Eva.

"Yes, please."

"Well, wait here a second while I fetch
you my binoculars. You'll get a much
better, close-up view if you use them."

So Eva took the field glasses then
climbed the fence and trod carefully
through the long grass, trying out the
heavy binoculars as she went.

"Everything's blurred!" she murmured,
putting them to her eyes. Then she
twisted a metal disc and altered the
lenses so that the scene grew clear.

Zoom! The binoculars gave her a close-
up of the pond with its long, straight
reeds at the edge and small, rocky
island in the centre. "Wow!" Eva was
impressed.

From the middle of the field she could
easily pick out three Canada geese
standing on the island and a small, dark
moorhen paddling close by. She walked
steadily on, aiming the glasses at other
wildlife – a rabbit scuttling off across
the field, and up in the blue sky, a grey

pigeon and two black rooks soaring on an
air current.

*Hey, this is what it must be like to make films
about wildlife!* Eva thought. She swung back
to the pond and saw three more moorhens
in the shallow water, swimming amongst
the reeds. *This is exciting!*

Two geese swam into view from round
the back of the island. That made five
altogether. Eva crept closer, then settled by
the edge of the pond. From this distance
she could make out the long black necks
and brown speckled wings of the geese.
*Just think, if this was Africa, I'd be looking at
pink flamingos! Or I could go to India and film
tigers!* She zoomed in on the moorhens.

*That's it, I'm going to be a wildlife
film-maker when I grow up!*

Eva's imagination took off and soared as

high as the rooks overhead. It was only when she spotted her first duck that she came back to earth.

It was the drake with his bright blue-green neck feathers and white collar, his plumage shining in the sunlight.

Perfect! Eva thought, holding her breath.

Then came the female – dowdier, plump and proud, with her head up, swimming out from behind the island after the drake.

OK, where are the ducklings? Eva kept her binoculars fixed on the spot. One duckling swam into view, bright yellow and perky. Then the second, bold and happy. The third took his time, but finally swam out from behind the rock. *Mum, Dad, ducklings one, two and three.*

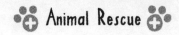

"Come on, Dilly!" Eva murmured. With binoculars steady in her hands, she waited a long time for her fluffy favourite to appear. And waited. And waited.

Chapter Seven

Friday, 18th. ***Dilly's got lost.
She's gone missing.*** I borrowed
Miss Eliot's binoculars and waited
by the pond for ages. There was no
sign of her.

Eva sat with the rescue centre's laptop
on her knees. She'd written the truth and
now it hit her really hard.

Her mum came into the bedroom to

ask her to turn off her light. "Everything OK?" she asked.

With tears in her eyes, Eva shook her head. She sniffed and pointed to the words she'd written.

Heidi read the blog. "Ah," she said softly, and sat on the bed. "Would you like to talk about it?"

"Dilly's got herself lost," Eva sniffed. "She was always struggling to keep up with the others and now they've gone off and left her!"

Her mum nodded. "That often happens with the smallest of the brood," she reminded Eva. "It's a question of strength and agility."

"But how could they leave her behind?" Eva pictured the dithery duckling's attempts to climb the slope

84

on to the golf course – how she flapped her tiny, flightless wings and struggled through the long grass while the others marched ahead.

Heidi waited a while before she answered. "It's how animals survive in the wild," she explained. "If they come up against a danger, their instinct is to get out as fast as they can. Only the fittest survive."

"So something bad happened – a fox, like you said before, or a car on Main Street – and the mum and dad just gave up on Dilly!"

Heidi nodded. "It sounds harsh, but that's what happens, I'm afraid. And we have to accept these things."

Eva was still stuck with the picture of Dilly hopping and bobbing, paddling and swimming in the river – a helpless, yellow ball of fluff. "Well, I haven't given up!" she said stubbornly.

Her mum put an arm round her shoulder and gave her a hug. "So what next?" she asked.

Now suddenly Eva knew exactly what she was going to do. She closed the laptop and snuggled under her duvet. "It's Saturday tomorrow," she murmured.

"I'm going to go out first thing in the morning to look for Dilly!"

Eva got up early as promised. She dressed and put on her trainers ready to go out and start her search.

There's no point going back to the pond at Swallow Court, she thought, skipping breakfast and setting off on foot in the direction of the river. *I spent ages there yesterday with the binoculars, and there was definitely no sign of her.*

So Eva decided to search the riverbank, close to where she'd first seen Dilly.

She crunched across pebbles and poked amongst tall reeds without finding anything. Then she crossed the stone bridge and started to look among the bushes at the edge of the golf course.

"Hey, you there, what do you think you're doing?" a voice called.

Eva glanced up to see an angry golfer walking towards her.

"Don't you know you're trespassing?" the man shouted.

Reluctantly Eva broke off her search. "I'm trying to find a lost duckling," she explained. "Her name's Dilly. She got separated from her family."

"That doesn't alter the fact that you're on private property," he argued. "What's more, you just put me off my game!"

Sighing, Eva retreated back over the bridge. She wandered further along the bank. "Where are you, Dilly?" she murmured, crouching to peer under the low branches of a willow tree. "Please don't hide. It's me – Eva. I'm your friend!"

But there were no answering cheeps, and no sign of the little lost duckling.

So Eva trudged back home, her head

hanging, her spirits low. It was almost ten o'clock when she reached the house and the phone was ringing. Eva ran to answer it.

It was Miss Eliot. "Is that Eva?" she asked hurriedly. "I'm glad I've caught you."

"What's wrong?" Eva could tell from the old lady's voice that something bad had happened. Maybe Tigger was ill. "Is everything OK?" she asked.

"No, dear, I'm afraid it's not!" Miss Eliot answered. "It's Tigger…"

Just as Eva had thought! "Is he hurt? Shall I get Mum?" she cut in.

"No, wait a moment. I'm looking out of my window to make sure. Yes, I was right. Tigger is chasing a yellow bird in my garden and I'm too slow to stop him!"

"Is it a duckling?" Eva asked, her heart thumping, dreading the answer.

"I'm not absolutely sure," Miss Eliot reported breathlessly. "I can't see it clearly. I just caught a glimpse. Wait – Tigger is prowling across the lawn as we speak. He's definitely stalking—"

"Is it Dilly?" Eva interrupted.

"Come here, Tigger, you naughty boy!" Miss Eliot's voice grew fainter, then she came back to the phone. "Yes, it's definitely a duckling," she admitted. "You'd better come quickly, Eva, if you want to save your little friend!"

Chapter Eight

Miss Eliot greeted Eva at her garden gate. "I'm so sorry!" she gasped.

Eva's heart missed a beat. She was too late. It was all over and Tigger had done his worst!

"I can't stop Tigger chasing birds. It's a dreadful habit, I know!"

"Where is he?" Eva asked, bracing herself for what she would find.

"In the back garden, prowling amongst the rose bushes. I can't see the duckling…"

Eva nodded. There was still hope then. She sprinted round the side of the bungalow to find the tabby cat crouched low on the ground, staring intently into the thick hedge beyond the roses.

"Shoo!" Eva cried, waving her arms and rushing at Tigger.

The cat twitched his tail but didn't take his eyes off the hedge.

"Go away! Shoo!" Eva yelled.

Tigger looked round. He glared angrily at Eva for disturbing him.

Meanwhile, there was a tiny movement from underneath the hedge and Eva saw a speck of yellow between the green leaves.

Tigger turned back towards the hedge and pounced.

"Stop!" Eva cried. She realized there

was nothing for it but to make a dive and grab the cat.

So as Tigger vanished under the hedge, Eva also pounced. Rose thorns pricked her bare wrists as she threw herself forwards. The landing was hard, but she barely felt it. "Got you!" she muttered as she seized Tigger and drew him out from the bottom of the hedge.

"Well done! Good girl!" Miss Eliot clapped her hands.

Taking a deep breath, Eva quickly handed a squirming Tigger to the old lady. Then she went down on her hands and knees and crawled back under the hedge. "So this is where you got to, Dilly!" she murmured, parting the slim branches and catching sight of the tiny duckling cowering in the shadows.

Cheep-cheep-cheep! Dilly scrambled amongst the tangled roots, out of Eva's reach.

"Don't worry, I'm not going to hurt you," she promised, stretching forwards to cup the duckling between her hands.

But Dilly didn't understand. Scared out of her wits by the fierce cat, all she wanted to do was run and hide.

She struggled deep into the hedge and
disappeared again.

"Come back," Eva pleaded, hearing
Miss Eliot take Tigger inside the house.
"Don't run away. You're safe now. I'm
here to take you back to your family!"

Back to the pond at Swallow Court, to
her brothers and sisters and the safety of
her mum and dad.

Gently, Eva parted more branches.
Her wrists were specked with blood from
the rose thorns and beginning to sting.

"Eva, what on earth are you doing?"

Annie's voice interrupted Eva's careful
search. She sounded like her mother in
a bad mood. Without answering, Eva
carried on looking for Dilly.

"Eva, I can see your legs and feet,
so I know you're under there!" Annie

96

insisted. "I saw you sprint off down Main Street. I followed to find out what you were up to."

"Be quiet, Annie!" Eva hissed. Every second that passed meant she had less chance of saving Dilly. By now she'd totally lost sight of the duckling and was starting to fear that she'd disappeared for good.

"But you have to tell me what happened." In her own way, Annie was as stubborn as Eva. "Come out. I want to know."

It was Miss Eliot who hurried out of the house to explain. "Tigger was stalking Eva's missing duckling. We almost had a disaster on our hands."

"Sshh!" Eva pleaded. All this talking was bound to scare Dilly away.

Miss Eliot lowered her voice to a whisper. "I brought the binoculars in case they help," she said, handing them to Annie. I'll go back inside and make sure Tigger doesn't try to escape."

Annie nodded. "Can you see Dilly?" she asked Eva quietly.

"No. She was here a few moments ago," Eva sighed. Her arms were really hurting now and her hair was getting caught in twigs. "Ouch! Hang on, I'll have to take a rest."

She emerged from the bushes, a bedraggled mess.

Eva picked the leaves off her jumper, noting Annie's smoothly brushed hair and whiter than white T-shirt. "She was here, but I think I lost her," she admitted miserably.

"Let me look," Annie offered, handing Eva the binoculars and crawling through the rose bushes. She peered into the dark undergrowth. "Nothing," she reported at last, emerging with tousled hair and grey dirt on her T-shirt.

Eva raised her eyebrows. Now they both looked a mess.

Annie sighed and wiped her hands on her T-shirt. Then she noticed Miss Eliot holding Tigger under her arm and tapping at the window.

"Come quickly!" the old lady mouthed through the glass.

The girls ran to the back door to be met by an agitated Miss Eliot.

"I've spotted the duckling!" she gasped. "Out on the pavement in front of the house next door. Once Tigger was out of the way, she must have fled across my neighbour's garden. She's heading for Main Street!"

Eva didn't stop to think. She simply ran out on to the crescent and picked up the search. "Dilly!" she shouted, running up the street, hoping yet fearing to find the duckling going walkabout. So much unknown danger, so many disasters waiting to happen in the big wide world!

"Dilly!" she called again as she reached Main Street and stopped by the sign reading SLOW DOWN – DUCKS CROSSING!

Annie sprinted to join her. "It's practically deserted," she gasped, looking both ways and praying that cars didn't speed by.

In the distance a tractor trundled up

the street. Pete Knight was out walking
Mitch. He gave the girls a wave.

"Hey, Pete, have you seen a stray
duckling?" Eva called, not knowing
which way to turn.

The joiner thought for a moment. "I
was going to say no, but come to think
of it, maybe we did."

Eva and Annie ran up to him. "How come?" Annie asked.

"I just had to give Mitch a stern talking to," Pete explained. "He was all for chasing off down the lane at the side of your place, Eva. I wanted him to keep going straight ahead. It's a good job I had him on the lead."

Eva glanced down at the lively terrier and gave him a pat. "So?" she asked.

"So I wondered what was so interesting down the lane and took a quick look. I didn't see anything, but I reckon it could have been a small animal or a bird that Mitch had spotted. Maybe even your duckling."

"Right, thanks, Pete. Come on, Annie!" Eva didn't wait to hear more. It was the only lead they had and she was determined to follow it.

"Are you thinking what I'm thinking?" Annie asked breathlessly as they sped down the narrow lane.

Eva nodded. "It would make sense for Dilly to make her way back to the river, wouldn't it? I mean, she'd recognize Main Street and the turn off down this lane. She'd be thinking she might find her mum and dad down here."

"Poor thing!" Annie gasped. She glanced helplessly in the long grass. "Maybe we should slow down and take a closer look?"

"You do that. I'll run on ahead to search by the river."

Eva sprinted on with the binoculars until she reached the riverbank. She kept a sharp lookout every step of the way but saw no sign of the yellow duckling. *So many places to hide!* she thought, almost overcome by the difficulty of the search. *One tiny duckling, one great big countryside!*

Stopping by the bend in the river, Eva raised the binoculars and focused them. Soon she could pick out pink wild flowers growing on the banks and individual pebbles on the shore.

She scanned the scene for a long time. Behind her she could hear Annie's footsteps drawing near.

"Anything?" Annie called.

"Nothing so far. How about you?"

"Zilch. It's a long way down that path. Do you think Dilly would get this far?"

Eva nodded. "She's done it once already."

"But not by herself."

"I know. Wait a sec." Eva steadied the binoculars. Across the far side of the river she spotted a pair of ducks swimming out from the bank. "See over there!" she told Annie. Could it be Dilly's mum and dad, back in their old stretch of river to search for their missing duckling?

The ducks swam boldly midstream.

No, they wouldn't leave their other babies, Eva thought. The binoculars brought out every detail of the drake's shining neck feathers and yellow beak, even his beady eyes.

"Look." Annie pointed to the bank. "Here come the ducklings!"

One – two – three – four ... five! Annie

and Eva held their breaths and counted.

The speckled ducklings headed straight for their parents until the whole family were happily bobbing in the rippling water.

"These are the ducks that chased Dilly's family away," Eva muttered. She lowered the field glasses then handed them to Annie.

It took Annie a while to get used to them. At first all she saw was a blur of sky and grass. Then she got the hang of it. "Wow, that's clear!" she said.

But Eva didn't hear her. She'd wandered off down to the pebbly shore and was looking left and right, feeling almost hopeless when it happened. "Oh!" she gasped.

"What?" Annie asked, turning sharply.

"Stop there, don't scare her!" Eva
hissed.

She hadn't believed it at first, but now
she was sure – a tiny yellow creature
had emerged from the long grass on to
the grey pebbles. It was hopping and
scrambling towards the water with a
faint cheeping sound.

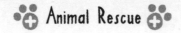

Annie stopped and stared.

"Dilly duckling!" Eva murmured with a sudden surge of hope. "You're amazing. You made it back to the river all by yourself. Well done!"

Chapter Nine

Dilly fluttered clumsily towards the river.

Eva and Annie watched in helpless silence.

"What do we do?" Annie whispered.

Eva shook her head. "I don't know. If we make a move, we'll scare her," Eva muttered under her breath.

"She's all alone," Annie said softly. "Oh look, she's starting to swim towards the other ducks!"

"They won't want her," Eva predicted. "She doesn't belong to them, and Mum said that ducks are very territorial."

Sure enough, as Dilly swam bravely out into the strong current, the mother duck spied her and gave a warning quack. The dad circled around his babies and gathered them in a tight knot.

"Come back, Dilly!" Annie begged.

But the little lone duckling swam on.

Quack! The mother duck's warnings grew louder. She swam towards Dilly, who was still struggling against the current. Then she stopped and trod water, watching carefully.

Cheep-cheep! Little Dilly swam right up to the female duck, asking to be taken in.

Quack! The angry mother stabbed at

Dilly with her broad beak to chase her away.

"Oh, that's cruel!" Annie cried.

"Dilly, come back here," Eva begged.

But Dilly tried again – swimming up close and dodging the stabbing beak, coming back a third time and being chased away.

"It's awful!" Eva murmured. "You'd think the mother duck would take pity on Dilly!"

"Sad!" Annie cried.

"Who's sad?" Karl interrupted. He'd been walking along the riverbank with the old Labrador, Val, when he'd spotted the girls. "What are you two up to?"

"It's Dilly!" Eva pointed to the middle of the river, where the female duck was still angrily sending the duckling away. "She's desperate for this other family to adopt her, but they're shooing her off. Look, now the male duck's joining in!"

"That's not good." Karl frowned. "Let me send Val in to scare the adults."

He didn't wait for Eva and Annie to make up their minds. Instead, he picked up a stout stick and threw it into the river for the Labrador. "Val, fetch!" he ordered.

The dog plunged into the water and swam strongly after the stick. As soon as the ducks saw her, they quacked and quickly turned tail.

"Don't hurt Dilly!" Eva cried after Val.

Dilly was stranded mid-river, paddling bravely but making no headway. Meanwhile, the unwelcoming ducks had fled to the far bank.

"Good girl, Val!" Karl called. "Hey, look at them scoot!"

"That's enough," Annie said. "Call Val back before she grabs one of them."

Karl nodded. "OK. Here, Val!"

The obedient Labrador turned tail and paddled back to the riverbank, while lonely Dilly seemed to give up the struggle at last and allowed herself to be carried downstream.

Just then, another duck appeared, flying low along the course of the river, under the arch of the stone bridge.

"Hey!" Eva pointed. She took the binoculars from Annie and tried to focus on the new arrival, but the duck was quickly out of sight. *I wonder!*

There was no time to stop and think. Dilly was being swept away towards the bridge.

"Let's run down there," Karl decided. "Maybe Dilly will manage to get back on to the bank where the river bends and we can rescue her."

As he sprinted off with Val, Eva and Annie decided to follow. "I feel so sorry for Dilly!" Annie muttered. "I've got an awful feeling she's not going to make it."

"Don't say that!" Eva pleaded, as she ran along the bank, watching Dilly bob and turn in the swirling water.

Karl and Val were ahead, leaning over the bridge, watching the duckling come towards them. As Annie and Eva drew level with Dilly, they saw her begin to swim again and fight the current. Gradually she made progress towards their bank.

"See, she's a little fighter!" Eva said.

And now the same new duck was flying back, swooping low, skimming the surface of the water as it slowed and flew smoothly under the old bridge, quacking to draw the tiny duckling's attention.

Dilly looked up and cheeped loudly.

The duck flew past, then with a tilt of

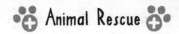
her strong wings she turned and came
back yet again.

Dilly swam towards the pebbles
where Annie and Eva stood. Both girls
held their breath. From the bridge Karl
crossed his fingers and watched.

Swoop! Splash! The duck landed in the water with a trail of spray. She swam right up to Dilly, bundling her out of the water on to the shore, fussing and flapping her wings as if to say, *There you are, you silly girl! I thought I told you never to leave my side!*

"It's Dilly's mum!" Annie cried in total joy. "She came back to find her baby!"

On the bridge Karl smiled and nodded.

Eva stared at Dilly and her mother, too choked up to say a single word.

Chapter Ten

<u>Saturday, 19th.</u> ...And guess what - mother duck marched Dilly up the riverbank and straight up the lane! There was just this bossy female and one tiny duckling making their way between the hedges like little soldiers on the march, left-right-left.

We followed them every step of the way, but the two ducks took no notice. On they went up by the side of Animal Magic on to Main Street, past the DUCKS CROSSING! sign, and left into Swallow Court. Miss Eliot was gobsmacked when she saw it. She'd been waiting at her window all that time, making sure that Tigger didn't get out and cause more trouble.

But Dilly and her mum didn't stop. They waddled across the garden and under the fence, right across the field. We could just see the mum's head popping up over the grass. (We had to keep a safe distance so as not to scare them.) The best bit was when they reached their pond. Daddy Duck spotted them and came waddling through the reeds. The other ducklings followed and they all rushed up to Dilly. Quack, quack, welcome back!

Dilly was nearly knocked flat, they were so excited. And they all gathered round and made a big fuss and we were watching and Annie cried a bit, and I sniffed but I didn't cry. Even Karl was choked.

Eva's hands hurt from typing so much so she stopped. Out of her bedroom window she saw Linda Brooks and Miss Eliot come into the yard with Annie. The evening shadows were long. Mickey let out an ear-splitting *EE-AW!*

Something's going on, Eva thought, leaving her diary and rushing down.

"Hey, Eva, Miss Eliot would like to talk to your mum," Annie said. "Is she around?"

"She's in the stables with Dad and Karl," Eva replied.

"And I wouldn't mind a tiny peep at your little Shetland pony," Linda Brooks added. "Annie tells me she's very sweet."

"Of course! Come in." Happily, Eva led the way.

Inside the stables they found Karl mucking out Mickey's stall, and Heidi and Mark busy working on Rosie's hooves. While Mark worked with a strong pair of clippers, Heidi smoothed the hooves with a file. Meanwhile, Rosie stood with her nose in her hay net, contentedly chewing.

Heidi was the first to look up and greet the visitors. "Hello, Linda. Hello, Miss Eliot, what a nice surprise!"

The old lady smiled broadly. "I expect you heard about the drama down by the pond?"

"We heard all right!" Mark lowered Rosie's hoof and grinned. "Eva hasn't stopped talking about it since!"

"She was splendid!" Miss Eliot insisted. "So were Karl and Annie. And so are you, Heidi. And Mark, of course."

"Hear, hear!" Linda added quietly.

Then she blushed. "Lovely little pony,"
she said, changing the subject.

Ee-aw! Mickey brayed.

"Not forgetting the beautiful donkey,"
Miss Eliot conceded.

There was silence for a while except
for the rasp of Heidi's file against Rosie's
hoof. Then the old lady slipped her hand
into her jacket pocket and spoke again.

"I have something for you," she said shyly, offering Heidi a long slip of paper.

Heidi came to the door and took it. "It's a cheque!"

Eva glanced at Karl and Annie, who shrugged. *Don't ask me!*

Heidi read the numbers. "A cheque for a very large amount of money," she gasped. "Made out to Animal Magic!"

"For you and your wonderful rescue centre!" Miss Eliot insisted. "And for all the good work you do."

Mark came across and looked at the cheque over Heidi's shoulder. He shook his head in astonishment. "This means we can pay our overdue bills and carry on without worrying about money for a long time to come," he said.

Eva, Karl and Annie stared at Miss Eliot.

"Are you sure about this?" Heidi asked, holding out the cheque as if offering it back.

Of course she's sure! Eva thought, quick as a flash.

Miss Eliot pushed the cheque away again. "Since I sold the manor house, I have more money than I'll ever need for myself," she insisted. "It would please me beyond words to make this donation."

"Take it!" Linda urged.

And so it was agreed. Animal Magic Rescue Centre could carry on matching the perfect pet with the perfect owner!

"That will be a giant pizza and death-by-chocolate all round!" Mark promised. "I feel another celebration coming on!"

EE-AW! Mickey said.

Rosie gave Mark a little don't-forget-me shove from behind and everyone laughed.

"Gorgeous little thing!" horse-mad Linda murmured, offering Rosie a mint from her pocket. "I wonder," she said softly with a faraway look in her eye.

"I wonder if there's room in my field for one adorable Shetland pony…"

ANIMAL + RESCUE

The Runaway Rabbit

Out now!

TINA NOLAN